A Teddy Bear's Christmas Carol

Starring Ebearnezer Bear

Based on *A Christmas Carol* by Charles Dickens

Adapted by Jill Wolf
Illustrated by Nancy Herndon

Copyright © 1986 Antioch Publishing Company
ISBN 0-89954-732-X
Made in the United States of America

Antioch Publishing Company
Yellow Springs, Ohio 45387

Ebearnezer Bear was the grouchiest old teddy bear there ever was. He was so grouchy, he didn't even like Christmas! When someone said, "Merry Christmas," Ebearnezer growled, "Bah, humbug!"

Ebearnezer owned a big bank and he was very rich, but he never gave anything to the poor. He hardly paid his bank clerk, Bear Cratchit, enough to buy a jar of honey. Cratchit had a large family to take care of, especially Tiny Ted, who had a broken leg.

But Ebearnezer didn't care about anyone's family, even his own. When his nephew asked him to come for Christmas dinner, Ebearnezer roared, "Bah, humbug!"

Then one Christmas Eve something happened to Ebearnezer Bear. When he went home to his dark, empty house, he thought he saw the ghost of his old friend Jacob Bearly at the front door.

But it disappeared and Ebearnezer hurried upstairs to his bedroom. Then the doorbell and the telephone began to ring at the same time. They rang and rang.

Next Ebearnezer heard someone (or something!) coming up the stairs, dragging heavy chains. By now, he was *really* scared!

The ghost of Jacob Bearly came right *through* the closed door! He was covered with keys, chains, locks, and money boxes and rattled with every step he took.

"What do you want, Jacob?" cried Ebearnezer. "You look so strange!"

"I have come to tell you to change your greedy, selfish ways," replied Jacob Bearly in a loud voice. "It is not too late *for you*. But first, 3 more ghosts must visit you."

"Oh, please, do they have to?" asked Ebearnezer.

Jacob Bearly rattled his chains. "Yes, they must. Do you want to end up *like me*?" With that, the ghost walked backwards to the window, which opened for him. He floated out and flew away into the night.

"Oh, dear," said Ebearnezer, still shaking with fear. He went to bed and pulled the covers over his head, hoping it had all been a bad dream. "Maybe it was that pizza I ate for supper," he told himself. But at one o'clock, he woke up to find a different ghost standing by his bed.

"I am the Ghost of Christmas Past. Come with me!" said the ghost. Ebearnezer took hold of its white robe and they flew back in time to Ebearnezer's childhood.

Ebearnezer saw his old grade school. Inside was a lonely little teddy bear who had been left behind during Christmas vacation. "Why, that's me!" cried Ebearnezer.

Then the ghost took Ebearnezer to the first place where he had worked. There was a very merry Christmas party going on and even Ebearnezer was having fun.

He was dancing with his first and only love, a beautiful teddy bear named Belle. She never married Ebearnezer because he loved making money more than he loved her. He remembered her and felt sad.

"I don't want to see any more! Take me home!" he told the ghost. Then Ebearnezer awoke again in his own king-size bed.

There was a bright light in the bedroom across the hall. He went in and saw a fat, jolly ghost wearing a green robe and a holly wreath. "I am the Ghost of Christmas Present," he said. "I will show you how everyone is celebrating Christmas this year."

First the ghost took Ebearnezer to a home on the poor side of town. "Why, it's Bear Cratchit's family," said Ebearnezer. "They're having Christmas dinner."

But it was not a very big dinner. The turkey was too small for such a large family of bears. Still, they all looked as if they loved each other and everyone was having fun—even Tiny Ted, whose brothers and sisters had drawn silly pictures on his cast to make him laugh.

Next the ghost took Ebearnezer to his nephew Fred's home. Fred's family and friends were playing trivia games and having a wonderful time at their Christmas party.

Then the ghost showed Ebearnezer two young teddy bears on the street. "Who are they?" Ebearnezer asked, for the little bears looked cold, hungry, and sick. "These are the poor that no one helped this Christmas," replied the ghost.

The Ghost of Christmas Present left Ebearnezer all alone then. He was tired of traveling, but there was one more ghost to come. It came quietly, dressed in a dark robe.

Ebearnezer followed the ghost to a city street. Two bears who knew him were talking about him. "Ebearnezer Bear got just what he deserved, the selfish old grouch!" said one bear and the other bear laughed, not in a very nice way either.

Finally the ghost led Ebearnezer to his office at the bank. Ebearnezer looked at the spot where his name used to be painted on the door. It was *gone* and a new name had appeared.

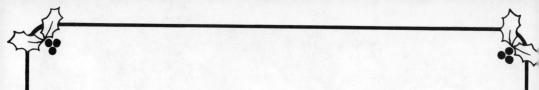

"Will I be unhappy and lose everything, even my bank, if I keep on being so selfish and mean? Oh, tell me this won't happen!" Ebearnezer begged the ghost. "Are you the Ghost of What Will Be, or can these awful things be changed?"

The ghost said nothing and Ebearnezer grabbed at it. Then suddenly he awoke in his own bed again.

It was daylight. Ebearnezer jumped out of bed and ran to the window. He saw a young teddy bear in the street and opened the window. "Tell me, what day is this?" he asked.

"It's Christmas Day!" said the teddy bear, looking up in surprise at Ebearnezer Bear.

"Good. I haven't slept through it. I have a lot to do today to make up for other Christmases," said Ebearnezer. "I've learned my lesson."

"Do you feel alright, mister?" the young bear asked and Ebearnezer laughed.

"Fine, thank you," he replied. "Could you run to the store down the street, buy a big turkey, and charge it to Ebearnezer Bear's account? If you're back in 15 minutes, I'll give you a big tip."

"Yes, sir!" shouted the teddy bear and ran down the street as fast as he could. When he returned, pulling the big turkey on his sled, Ebearnezer went out and gave the young teddy a twenty-dollar tip!

"Take the turkey to Bear Cratchit and his family," Ebearnezer said and gave the address. He smiled to himself, for he felt happier than he had in years. He wanted to dance and sing and celebrate Christmas forever.

Ebearnezer put on his best clothes and went to his nephew's house. When Fred saw Ebearnezer, he was glad his uncle had come. They had dinner, then played trivia games with Fred's family and friends. Ebearnezer had a great time—he even laughed when he gave the wrong answers to the questions!

Everyone who knew the old Ebearnezer Bear was surprised at the change in him. After that one special Christmas Eve, Ebearnezer always gave money to the poor. There was no one who celebrated Christmas as much as he did.

He gave Bear Cratchit a big raise and helped take care of his family. Tiny Ted's leg got better and he walked without crutches or a cast.

The Cratchits were very glad and grateful that everything turned out so well. As Tiny Ted often cried, "God bless us, *every one!*"

The End